Short Stories

Asten Clarke

Copyright © 2021 Asten Clarke
All rights reserved

ISBN: 9798516280214

More by Asten Clarke

Rainbow Balloons

The Popper: Mark's Story

The Fan

Fan Friction

Star Struck

Who Am I?: An Autism and BPD Story

Social Media:

Instagram: @astenclarkewriter

Twitter: @AstenWriter

www.astenclarke.com

www.rainbowballoonsbooks.com

A Library Romance

Bonnie Walters scanned through the books on the shelves. The library was her favorite place to be, and there were usually the same faces at the library every single day. Bonnie had friends here - in fact, in was the only place she really had any friends.

Today, Bonnie was in the mood for some light romance. She scanned the shelves once more, before deciding on a book she'd never heard of, but it sounded good.

"*Midnight Bride* by Blanche Raven," she read aloud to herself, but quietly, of course. She took the book up to the counter to get it stamped.

As she was walking up to the counter, someone else hurried in front of her.

"Excuse me," said Bonnie, tapping on the man's shoulder, "but I believe I was first in the queue."

The man turned around, and Bonnie was immediately taken by his sparkling brown eyes.

"I'm sorry," said the man. "Would you like to go in front of me?"

Bonnie nodded, and pushed in front of the man, who was watching her the whole time she was getting her book checked out. It was a little unnerving, to say the least.

Bonnie turned around again after having her book checked out. She once again looked into those sparkling eyes. "Sorry," she said, "what was your name?"

"I'm Ryan," the man said."Do you come here often?"

Bonnie laughed. What a cheap chat-up line. "If you must know," she said, "I'm here every day. Almost, anyway."

"Well, then I am too," said Ryan.

Bonnie didn't quite know what to say. She repositioned her bag on her shoulder to make it more comfortable. "Are you sure about that?"

"Absolutely," Ryan said.

"In that case, Ryan, I guess I'll see you tomorrow." She grabbed her book and left.

###

The next day, Ryan arrived at the library before Bonnie did. Bonnie was almost surprised to see him there when she got there.

"I told you I'd be here," said Ryan, smiling.

"Yes you did," Bonnie said.

"So," Ryan said, sitting down in front of her. "How was that book?"

"How do you know I've read any of it?"

"You seem like the type of girl to start reading a book as soon as she gets one."

"Very good, Ryan." Bonnie was almost surprised, but then again, she did think of herself as a little predictable.

"So, how was it?" asked Ryan.

"It was... different to most other romance books I've read."

"How so?"

Bonnie sighed. "Well, it was very... fast paced, and... dark."

"Sounds very interesting."

Bonnie nodded. "It is. I haven't finished it yet."

"Well, it'll have to wait. I'd like to take you somewhere less... quiet."

Bonnie was shocked. "You'd like to take me on a... date?"

"Don't think of it as a date. Think of it as two friends having a catch up."

"But I hardly know you."

"But you will, if you meet me for a catch up." He gave her a piece of paper with a long number written on it. "That's my phone number. Call me."

Bonnie wondered why he couldn't have just put his number in her phone like a normal person.

###

It took a good few days before Bonnie plucked up the courage to call Ryan, but when she did, they arranged to meet at a cafe the following day.

Bonnie stirred her tea as she looked into Ryan's eyes once more. Something about his eyes amazed her.

She thought for a moment he'd caught her staring and ended up giggling like a school girl as she looked away.

"So," Ryan said, "how come you're at the library so much?"

"What can I say?" said Bonnie. "I love books."

"How many do you think you've read this year?"

"Too many to count. What were you doing in the library anyway?"

"I had to take a couple of books back for my dad. I'm so glad I came in that day. I mean, I could've come in *any* day and still see you."

"That's true. But why do you like me so much?"

Ryan leaned back in his chair. "There's just something about you. I can't put my finger on it."

"Funny, that's how I feel about you." Bonnie took a sip of her drink.

"So, shall I meet you at the library tomorrow?"

"I guess so," said Bonnie. They finished their drinks and parted ways.

###

Bonnie went to the library the next day as usual, but Ryan wasn't there. She waited a good few hours for him to arrive, but he didn't. She couldn't concentrate on the book she was reading. She couldn't help but wonder where he was. Was he blowing her off? Did he forget about her?

She decided to wait another hour before heading home. When she was home, she tried calling Ryan but it went straight to voicemail. Very weird indeed.

###

Bonnie woke the next day to her doorbell going off. She threw some clothes on, ran downstairs and answered the door. It was Ryan. She could feel her heart flutter when she saw him there.

"What happened to you yesterday?" she asked.

"I wasn't sure you really liked me," said Ryan. "I was kind of testing you, I guess."

Bonnie sighed happily and put her arms around Ryan. "Don't you ever disappear on me again. Promise?"

Ryan kissed her softly. "Promise."

Amazing Saturday

Prologue

As a writer, I appreciate a good story. It can come from anywhere, real or not, fiction or non-fiction. But sometimes the best stories are the ones that are a hundred per cent real and true.

That's where my story comes in.

It all started one evening when I was writing a fan fiction story about the band, Amazing Saturday. You may have heard of them... Oh, who am I kidding? *Everyone* knows Amazing Saturday. They are quite possibly the biggest band in the universe. You see, I like Amazing

Saturday a lot. In fact, you could say I *loved* them. Actually, *obsessed* might be a better word. I'm not the usual type of girl to get obsessed over a boyband, but Amazing Saturday just tick all the boxes for me. I love their music, and their videos, and their personalities. Jenson, Justin, Alvin and Milo - they just gel so well together. They're the perfect band...

I realize I'm getting ahead of myself. So, anyway, like I said, I was writing some Amazing Saturday fan fiction. And Felix - that's my boyfriend - was reading it as I typed.

"Are all your stories about Amazing Saturday?"

I stopped typing, swiveled my chair round and looked at Felix. "Well,

I've never really thought about writing about anything else."

"You won't get published if all your stories are about this band." Felix crossed his arms.

To be honest, I'd never really thought about being published before. "I only write these stories for me," I said.

"Have you ever published them to any fan fiction sites?" Felix asked.

That didn't seem like a bad idea. I wouldn't mind getting some feedback for my writing, not to mention meeting other Amazing Saturday fans.

And so I posted a story to one of the most popular fan fiction sites. And that's how my Amazing Saturday adventure started...

One

Oak Park High School, the sign read. I stood there staring at it for a good few minutes as my fellow students buzzed back and forth around me. I wondered to myself if I'd dressed correctly, or if my hair was in place. I tucked a strand of long brown hair behind my ear, and made my way toward the entrance of the school.

The inside of the school was no less chaotic than the outside. Students scurried to their classrooms all around me I started feeling a little nauseous. My heart started pounding and I started to sweat. I'd never been to such a big school before. How would I cope?

"Hi," a girl said as she came up to me, catching me off guard. "You're new here, right?"

I nodded silently.

"I'm Ellis," she said, extending her hand for me to shake. At least, I think that was what she was doing.

I didn't take it though. "Lola," I said, warily.

Ellis finally put her hand down. I think she was disappointed."What brings you to Oak Park?"

I sighed, pulling my backpack further onto my shoulder. "My mom got a new job. We had to move."

"Where did you live originally?" She followed me as I walked toward my class.

What's with all the questions? I thought to myself.

Ellis didn't wait for an answer. "You're going to love it here at Oak Park."

I seriously doubted that. "It's just a school," I shrugged.

Finally, I made it to the outside of my class. "This is me," I said.

"See you at lunch," said Ellis as she walked away.

I shook my head, and walked into my class.

###

The first half of the day passed by in a blur. By the time lunch came around I was mentally exhausted from using my brain so much. Lunch was a very welcome break.

It didn't take long for Ellis to spot me. "Lola!" she called out to me in the cafeteria. I tried to pretend I hadn't seen her, but to no avail. She already knew I had seen her - and heard her.

Reluctantly I walked over to her table. She was sitting with a few other students, presumably her friends. Why she'd taken such an interest in me, I'll never know. Was she on some kind of new student welcoming committee?

I put my tray down on the table beside a spare seat.

"Guys, this is Lola," said Ellis. "She's new here."

"Hi." I waved to everybody at the table.

No one was really listening to me. They were all too busy on their phones.

Ellis cleared her throat loudly. I do wish she hadn't done that.

"Oh, hey," one of the girls turned around to say.

"That's Kira," Ellis told me. "She was new here too a couple of months ago."

Definitely on some kind of welcoming committee, I thought to myself.

"Tell us about yourself," said Kira.

"Uh..." I hesitated. "I'm originally from Warmsteam, I have a boyfriend named Felix, I love the band Amazing Saturday..."

"Amazing Saturday?" Ellis said. "Hmm. Not really my kind of music."

"Nor mine, usually, but I just love their sound."

"That's really interesting," said Kira.

Suddenly there was this girl walking through the cafeteria like she owned the place.

"Who's that?" I asked.

Ellis sighed. "That's Summer Monroe," she said. "Totally spoiled. We just try to avoid her."

"Although I think she likes Amazing Saturday," said Kira.

Ellis shot her a look that told her she was less than impressed.

"But it's best if you avoid her," Kira said quickly.

I made the decision to form my own opinion about her.

###

The next class of the day was science class, and who should sit down next to me but Summer Monroe.

"Hi," I said, nervously.

She said nothing.

"I heard you like Amazing Saturday."

Again, she said nothing. She flicked her long, blond hair and looked down toward the table.

Maybe Ellis and Kira were right about her?

Two

When I got home I was eager to log into my computer and see how my fan fictions were doing. I'd posted some of them to the official Amazing Saturday forums, and I was eager to see what other fans thought of them.

One of the comments on the fan fiction site read, *Very tame compared to other AS fan fiction I've read.*

Tame? What did that mean?

Suddenly there was a knock on my door. It was Felix.

"Thought I'd stop by and say hi."

I ran up to him and threw my arms around him.

"How was your first day at Oak Park?" he asked.

"Tiring," I said. "I made some friends. At least, I *think* I made some friends."

"You think?" he laughed.

I nodded. "How was your day?"

Felix still goes to my old school, Grand Ridge High. It's a little smaller than Oak Park.

"So-so," he said, sitting down on my bed. He saw that I was on the fan fiction site on my computer. "Got any comments yet?"

"I had one saying that my stories were 'tame'. What does that mean?"

Felix shrugged. "Beats me."

"Anyway, I'm feeling inspired. I'm going to write a new story."

"Now?"

I nodded.

"But I just got here!"

"You can sit and watch me."

He rolled his eyes and laid back on my bed.

###

The next day, school buzzed by in a blur again. Once more, I was eager to get home again, eager to see what had been happening on the Amazing Saturday forums, and the fan fiction sites. I had made a couple of friends on the forums, and added them on Facebook.

Suddenly a message popped up from one of my fellow fans, Amelia Swansons.

Have you heard the news? it read.

News? What news?

No I haven't, was my response.

Justin's left Amazing Saturday.

My blood ran cold.

Is this some kind of joke? I typed.

I wish it was, said Amelia. She attached a link to a news story about Justin leaving the band. I read the article in absolute horror.

What does this mean for the band? I asked.

Who knows? Amelia asked. *They're lacking in popularity anyway.*

That was true. Amazing Saturday were not as popular as they had been lately.

I think they might split, typed Amelia.

As you can imagine, this is not what I wanted to hear.

We have to do something, I said.

What can we do? Amelia asked. *We're just fans.*

Fans have got to have some kind of power, I typed. *We can't just sit back and do nothing.*

I don't see what good we could do.

But I wasn't giving up that easily. There had to be something I could do.

###

I tried not to think too much about what was going on with the band. I tried to focus on my writing, but as you can imagine, it was difficult. I wished I could write something else, something original. I wondered whether I should include Justin in my fanfics any more. Mind you, it was fiction. So anything could happen. I could write a story where Justin realizes his mistake and wants to re-join the band. Or maybe one where he never left at all.

I tried to shake off these thoughts. It would only make me sad if I thought about it too much.

"Knock-knock-knock."

I turned around. It was Felix knocking at my door. I ran up to him and threw my arms around him.

"I heard what happened with the band. Are you OK?"

"I think so," I said, "although this is really going to impact my fanfics."

"Maybe it's time to write something else," he said.

"I have thought about that."

"You need some inspiration. Let me help with that." He came up close to me and started kissing my neck. It made me feel a little uncomfortable.

"Felix, what are you doing?" I asked, pushing him away.

"What are *you* doing? I want to have some fun."

"Fun?"

He tried to kiss my neck again. He started to put his hand down my pants. I slapped his hand hard.

"Lola, what's wrong with you?"

I backed away. "Please don't do that again."

"You're ridiculous!" He got up, exited my bedroom and slammed the door behind him.

So now, not only was all this going on with the band, but Felix was mad at me, too.

Great.

Three

The next day at school I tried to concentrate, I really did, but I couldn't take my mind off of what was happening elsewhere. The issue with Felix last night had me shaken up, for sure, but the real reason I couldn't concentrate was that I was thinking about the band. I was thinking there must be something us fans could do to make things better for them. I didn't want them to split up. In fact that was the last thing I wanted. I knew there was something we could do.

I also knew that things would be a lot easier if there were another AS fan at school. That way we could hook up at lunch time and discuss what we could do for the band.

I knew I had to talk to Summer Monroe.

Luckily I had Science class again, and Summer would be sitting next to me. I just hoped I could get through to her this time.

She sat down next to me and flicked her long blond hair back over her shoulders. She looked downward, not meeting my gaze.

"Hi," I said. No response.

I tapped her on the shoulder. This time she turned around.

"What's your problem?" she asked.

"Nothing," I stammered. "I just wanted to talk to you because I know you like Amazing Saturday and-"

She sighed loudly. "Who told you this?"

"Ellis and Kira."

She laughed. "Why do you want to hang around with those two dorks?"

"I-I'm new here so I don't really know anyone."

She looked at me. "Listen, Lola. If you wanna be cool at this school, you shouldn't be hanging around with dorks like Ellis and Kira."

"Who should I be hanging around with?"

She thought for a moment. "Me."

"I thought you didn't like me."

"I don't know you," said Summer. "Now, what's this about Amazing Saturday? Do you like them?"

"I love them."

She smiled. "You have excellent taste."

"I just wanted to talk to you because I know they're having problems right now, and I wondered if there was something we could do."

"I don't see what we could do."

"That's exactly what my friend Amelia said online. But fans must have some kind of power."

"When you figure it out, let me know." She turned her back to me and started making notes in her notepad.

I felt very conflicted about Summer Monroe. Yes, she was a fellow AS fan, but it was like she didn't want to know me for some reason.

Still, I wasn't giving up on her that easily.

I got home and I was eager to get online again. When I did manage to log on, there was a message from my fellow fan, Emma Howard.

I still can't believe this is happening, it read. *I'm so worried about the future of the band.*

Don't panic, I wrote. By now I had decided what I wanted to do. *I'm going to arrange a celebration, to show them what they mean to us.* I'd written the words and hit 'send' before I'd realized what was happening.

That's a great idea, typed Emma. *I'll definitely be able to make it.*

You don't know what day it is yet.

It doesn't matter. I'd clear my entire schedule for Amazing Saturday.

Sometimes I thought Emma was a bigger fan than me. But that, I thought, was unlikely.

How are the fanfics going?

They've gone on the back burner a little. I'm too concerned about what's happening with the band, plus I've been having problems with Felix.

What kind of problems?

He tried it on with me the other day, and got a bit upset when I refused his advances.

Any reason why you refused them?

I didn't know there had to be a reason to refuse my boyfriend's sexual advances.

I'm just not ready.

How old are you again?

Seventeen.

Then Emma went a bit quiet. In fact, she didn't say another word to me for the rest of the night. The rest of the week, in fact.

I wonder what had gotten into her?

###

When I got to school the next day I went straight to the computer room. I inserted my memory stick into one of the computers, and printed off the poster I'd designed the night before. If I was going to host an Amazing Saturday celebration, I needed to get the word out somehow. Even if there were no other hardcore fans at my school, surely there must be some people who at least liked them, and wouldn't want to see them split?

"You're really going all out for this, aren't you?" Kira said to me as I was putting the posters up.

"Do you think it will work? I'd hate all that hard work to be for nothing," said Ellis.

"I have to try," I said.

"Just how is this going to work?" asked Kira.

"OK. We have the event, and hopefully that all goes smoothly. Hopefully there will be some kind of media coverage, and word will get out to the band, and then they will realize how much they mean to us, and hopefully Justin will re join the band, and everything will be great!"

"Sounds like you've got it all figured out," said Ellis.

"Yep, it's all worked out in my brain."

I just hoped it would work.

Four

I was in my bedroom putting the finishing touches to my plans for the celebration when Felix came in. As usual, I went up to him and threw my arms around him. He pulled me in close, and started running his hands up and down my body. It felt a little gross.

"What are you doing?"

"Getting you ready," he said.

"Ready for what?"

"You should know."

I was confused, to say the least. I backed away. "Felix, I'm busy right now organizing the celebration."

He stared deep into my eyes. "What's wrong with you?"

"Nothing. I'm busy. Leave me alone."

He once again left my room, slamming the door behind him.

I didn't bother going after him.

###

The next day at school I had science class again. And that meant sitting next to Summer Monroe.

This time, she actually spoke to me, instead of me talking to her.

"I just wanted you to know I think it's great what you're doing with the celebration and everything," she said.

"Oh, that," I said. I hadn't given much thought to it since Felix stormed out of my room last night. I was more worried about him than anything else. "Anyone else would have done the same thing." That wasn't strictly true, otherwise there would be hundreds of celebrations happening around the country. And as far as I was aware, mine was the only one happening.

"Do you think it will work?"

The amount of times I'd been asked that question...

"It has to," I said. "I don't have a Plan B."

"I hope it does work. For all of us."

I hoped it would work too.

###

When I got home from school I had a call from Famous Magazine. They'd heard about the celebration and wanted the scoop.

"So tell us how you think this is going to work," the woman on the other end of the phone said.

"OK. I'm hoping the band will get to know what I'm doing and see how much they mean to us," I said.

"That's really interesting. And how are you going to get the word out to them?"

"News travels fast in our age of social media," I explained. "I'll write a post on Facebook about it, make it public so people can share, and hopefully the word will get out that way."

"Thanks for talking to me today, Lola," the woman said.

I hung up.

Five

I was in my room doing some writing when Felix came in. As usual I ran up to him and put my arms around him. But he backed away.

"What's wrong?" I asked.

Felix sighed. "I need to talk to you."

I took his hand and led him over to my bed, and we sat down.

He sighed again."I think we should stop seeing each other."

My blood ran cold. "What? Why?"

"You're not giving me what I want."

"What do you want?"

"You don't know?"

"Not if you don't tell me."

He sighed once more, and hung his head. "I want to be intimate with you."

"I'm not ready yet."

"Lola, you're seventeen. If you're not ready now, when will you be ready?"

He got up and stormed out of my room.

I collapsed on the bed, crying my eyes out.

The next day at school I was meant to meet up with Summer to discuss the celebration, but my mind was elsewhere. Why did I have issues being intimate with Felix? Was there something wrong with me? Of course, this was all just hindsight now. Our relationship was over. But what if I could never be in another relationship again? What if I was never ready? What if no one wanted to know me because I wasn't ready? All these thoughts made me really sad. I felt like I was going to cry.

"Lola? Are you OK?"

I looked up and saw Summer standing there. How could Ellis and Kira not like Summer? She seemed perfectly decent to me.

"Yeah, I'm fine," I lied. I wiped my eyes and got my notepad out of my bag. I tried to focus on the celebration, but it was hard.

"You don't look fine," said Summer. She took a seat next to me. "Everything OK with your boyfriend?"

Hearing her say that made me feel like I was going to cry again. I pulled myself together. "My boyfriend broke up with me."

"Oh no, why?"

I didn't really want to tell Summer the reasons for our break-up. I was embarrassed. But I needed someone to vent to, and so I opened up.

I sighed deeply. "Felix wanted our relationship to progress physically, but I wasn't ready."

"Any particular reason you weren't ready?"

"I don't know; it's just something I've never really wanted to do."

"Maybe you should get yourself checked out. That's not normal."

Maybe it wasn't normal, but I was happy with the way I was. I was happy without all that sexual stuff in my life. Maybe, I thought, Felix breaking up with me was a good thing. Even if Summer didn't see things that way.

I decided to change the subject. "So, let's concentrate on the celebration."

But in the back of my mind I couldn't help wondering, maybe there *was* something wrong with me?

###

When I got to school the next day there was a load of commotion outside the school hall.

"What happened?" I asked.

"Vandalism," explained Mr Bowman, the headmaster. "Our handymen are working hard to fix the problem. It does mean, however, we'll have to cancel your little celebration."

My blood ran cold.

"I need to see the damage," I said. I barged past Mr Bowman and ran into the school hall. The whole hall was completely trashed. On the wall someone had written 'AMAZING SATURDAY SUCK' in graffiti. Obviously whoever did this did not want the celebration to take place.

Summer ran towards me. "I heard what happened and I came as quick as I could," she panted.

"What are we going to do now?" I asked.

"We'll have to check out some other venues and choose one."

"But the celebration is supposed to take place next weekend. We don't have time to find a replacement venue!"

"Leave this to me," said Summer. "I think I know what to do."

Six

When I got home I went straight online. A message popped up form Emma.

How's the celebration plans going?

Not good. Problems with the venue. But don't worry; my friend's on it. I couldn't believe I'd just referred to Summer Monroe as a 'friend'.

I hope it gets sorted out, said Emma. *So, did you sort out things with Felix?*

No. He broke up with me, I typed. I did wish people would stop asking me about Felix; it made me sad.

Why?

He wanted to do all this sexual stuff with me, and I don't want that.

You don't want it ever?

Probably not, I said.

Have you got yourself checked out or anything?

OK, that's the second time someone's said I needed to get 'checked out'. Maybe there *was* something wrong with me?

I decided to hit up Google to get some answers. I typed in *Don't want to be intimate with my boyfriend.* I spent the next hour going through all the results. One word kept coming up: *Asexual.*

I looked into an official looking site, which said that about one percent of the population is asexual, meaning they don't feel sexual attraction to anyone.

So that was that. I was asexual. There was nothing wrong with me! I felt so liberated. The more and more I read the more it sounded like me. I read that asexuals are sometimes called 'aces'. I liked the thought of referring to myself as ace. Very cool! I also felt relieved that there was nothing wrong with me, and there were others like me. Thousands of others, in fact.

Now I had my new identity, I could concentrate on the celebration.

###

Summer came up to me the next day with news about the venue for the celebration.

"My dad said we could use the community hall," she said. "He's booked it and everything."

"Cool," I smiled.

"You seem happy today," said Summer.

"You remember that Felix broke up with me for not doing sexual stuff with him?"

"Yeah, sorry about that."

"Don't be. Last night I made an amazing discovery. Turns out, I'm asexual."

"You're a sexual what?"

That made me laugh. "It means I don't feel sexual attraction, to anyone."

"Wow. I don't get it."

I was kind of expecting that. "I'll explain another time."

"OK. So you're never going to be with anyone?"

"I still feel romantic attraction, but not sexual."

She thought for a moment. "Yeah, I still don't get it."

"Never mind. Anyway, did you get all the posters changed with the correct venue for the celebration?"

And with that, we chatted about the celebration as we walked to our class.

###

At home a few days later, I decided to look more into this asexual stuff online.

I read that people have a sexual orientation and a romantic orientation. That made sense. I still wanted a romantic relationship with someone. I also read that the symbol for asexuality was cake, because cake is better than sex!

Suddenly my phone rang. It was Felix.

"I just wanted to see how you are," he said.

"But you broke up with me," I replied.

"Doesn't mean I can't still care about you," he said.

How sweet.

"So, what's new?"

"I figured out why I didn't want to do stuff with you. I'm asexual."

"What does that mean?"

"It means I don't feel sexual attraction to anyone."

"Right..." I could tell he didn't know what to say next. He changed the subject. "How's plans for the celebration going?"

"OK, I guess. We had some problems with the venue but that's all been solved now."

"Goos luck with everything."

Despite being a little sex crazed, Felix was really a good guy.

"Thank you. And I hope life's treating you kind as well." I hung up.

Seven

The day of the celebration had arrived. I was so excited I could barely control myself. We had chosen to hold the celebration on a Saturday (when else?) so I headed to the community hall early to supervise preparations. People were putting posters and balloons all over the place, and there were also people setting up music and food. The only band on the playlist was, of course, Amazing Saturday - their back catalog was extensive enough to cover the entire night.

A few hours later, the celebration was in full swing. Loads of people from school came, plus a few people I didn't recognize. They must have heard about the celebration via the forums.

It was my job to go round and talk to everyone. It was cool meeting fellow fans. They came from all walks of life. One of the fans sticks out in my mind, though. She was sitting on her own in the corner reading a book.

"Hi," I said, "I'm Lola."

"I'm Holly," she said.

"Are you sure you're OK?"

"Yep, fine."

"Are you a big fan of Amazing Saturday?"

Holly nodded. "But I'm not like other fans."

"How'd you mean?"

"I only like their music. I don't fancy any of them. I'm asexual."

My stomach did a little flip.

"Are you OK?" Holly asked.

"I'm asexual too!" I exclaimed.

"You're joking?"

I shook my head. "At least, I *think* I am."

"If you think you are, then you probably are," said Holly, and it was the most affirming thing I"d heard in recent times. I finally felt good about myself. I was asexual, and there was nothing wrong with that!

I spent the rest of the night chatting to Holly. She told me about some great forums to visit, and all sorts of stuff. I added her on Facebook also. I knew I'd made a friend for life.

###

The day after the celebration, I could not have been more exhausted.

Going around and talking to everyone all night had tired me out.

But I was eager to see the results of having the celebration, if any.

I logged on to Facebook to chat to my fellow fans.

Great party last night, typed Amelia.

I know, it was fantastic. I meant that in more ways than one. *Any news on the band?*

Actually there is, said Amelia. *The band are splitting up.*

My heart sank.

Is there anything we can do? I asked.

We've done all we can, said Amelia.

I closed my laptop lid, and sat it silence for a few moments.

After a few hours I was ready to go back online again. Holly was online.

I'm so sorry the celebration didn't work, she said.

It did work, I said. *Everyone had a fantastic time, and that's the important thing.*

Well done you for thinking positive, said Holly.

I'm trying. I sighed deeply as I typed. I really was trying to think positive. I was trying to convince myself that the celebration *was* a success. Which it was. And the most important thing was that I made a friend in Holly. And she helped me affirm my identity.

Amazing Saturday were no more. But Asexual Lola was just getting started.

Battle of the Bands

Georgia Lewis peered around the curtain. It looked like there were hundreds of people there, and they were all there to see her. OK, so maybe not *all* there to see her - it was the school talent show and Georgia and her friends had formed a girl band for the night. There were actually two bands going head-to-head tonight - Georgia's band, YEG (Yamsin, Evie and Georgia), and her arch nemesis Lulu Smith and her 'minions' Hannah and Chloe in their own band, 'Luluatron' (stupid name, thought Georgia. If they were being judged on names alone, YEG would win hands down.) There were other kids doing various different acts, but Georgia wasn;t too worried about them. The only really competition was Lulu and her henchwomen.

"I'm so nervous," Evie said, chewing on her nails slightly.

"Pull yourself together, Evie," Georgia scolded. "We've got this."

"Well, well, well," Lulu came over with her hangers-on. "If it isn't EGG." Hannah and Chloe giggled.

"It's YEG," Georgia explained, calmly. "What do you want?"

"Just eyeing up the competition." Lulu flicked her long blonde hair back as she looked Georgia and her friends up and down.

"There *is* no competition," Yasmin retorted.

"You're right," Lulu said, "I win hands down."

"What about u-" Hannah began.

Lulu put her hand up to shush her. "Shut up, Hannah."

"Yes, boss."

Lulu smirked.

The time was coming closer for Luluatron to perform. Georgia was looking forward to seeing how awful they were going to be.

"Please welcome - LULUATRON!" the teacher said over the microphone.

"Laters, losers," Lulu said, making an 'L' shape with her fingers as she walked onto the stage.

As Luluatron performed a 'cover' of the latest Taylor Swift hit, it sounded like three cats being strangled. Georgia plugged her ears, but she was laughing, *We've got this in the bag,* she thought, smiling.

The girls were practically booed off stage. If anyone in the audience was once a Swiftie, they sure as heck weren't any more. 'Murdered' wasn't even the word for what Luluatron did to that song.

"Er... thanks for that, Lulu," the teacher said as the girls exited the stage. "Next up, we have YEG! Am I saying that right?"

"That's us," said Evie.

"Come on, girls," said Georgia. "Let's be fabbity-fab with knobs on."

"Are you quoting those books again?" asked Yasmin.

"...Maybe," said Georgia.

As the girls headed for centre stage the nerves started to well up inside Georgia. But as soon as she started singing- a song she'd written herself - those nerves faded away. She was having the time of her life on that stage. And the audience seemed to be enjoying themselves too. Georgia loved every second of it. She wanted to do this for the rest of her life.

When the song was finished the crowd erupted into applause. The sound was deafening, but Georgia didn't care. She was in love with being on stage and singing.

The girls hurried backstage, and there were hugs and high-fives all around.

"We were awesome!" Yasmin screeched.

But not everyone agreed.

"You sounded like three babies screaming," Lulu smirked.

"Oh stop talking about yourself, Lulu," Evie said, and Yasmin and Georgia laughed.

Lulu whipped her blonde hair around her face and turned back to her henchwomen.

"Are we gonna win, boss?" asked Chloe.

"Duh, of course we are," said Lulu.

They wouldn't have to wait long to find out. The results were in.

"And the winner is.... YEG!"

The girls all clapped and cheered as their name was called.

But Lulu was not happy. "I'll get you back for this, Lewis!"

Georgia made the shape of an L and put it to her forehead. "LOSER!"

Sunshine's Tears

Once upon a time there was a lovely little princess named Sunshine Star. She had long blonde hair and blue eyes, and lived in the magical Kingdom of Netsa. With her bubbly attitude and ability to heal the depressed, Sunshine was loved by everyone who knew her... well, everyone except for Stone Woods, an evil witch who hated happiness.

But Sunshine had a dark secret - she was sometimes extremely unhappy, so much so that she would cry for the whole day. She could never tell anyone of her secret, for fear the evil witch might learn of it and take advantage.

The reason Stone Woods did not like happiness is because she was unhappy herself, but like Sunshine, she would never tell anyone. She wanted to be the happiest person in the kingdom, even though she was desperately sad.

One day Stone Woods was walking through the kingdom of Netsa and happened to come across Sunshine's house. Sunshine did not like to live in the castle because she wanted to live like a normal teenage girl. On this particular day, Sunshine was having a bad day, and was crying in her room. Her window was open and as she walked past, Stone Woods could hear her sobs. That gave her an idea for a wicked plan.

The next day, Stone Woods turned up at Sunshine's house, wearing a disguise. She was dressed as an old beggar woman. She knocked on the front door.

"Hello?" Sunshine asked brightly as she answered the door. She was extremely good at hiding her emotions from other people.

"Hello, dear," replied Stone Woods. "I was wondering if you had a place for me to stay? I'm homeless, you see."

The story pulled at Sunshine's heartstrings and being the kind princess she was, she said, "Of course. Come in."

"Thank you, dear, how long can I stay here?"

"As long as you like."

Perfect, thought Stone Woods.

So Sunshine and Stone Woods - still disguised as the old woman - fell into a routine of living together. But it had been a whole week and Stone Woods still hadn't seen Sunshine crying yet. She soon realised that Sunshine would only cry in private, and that she would have to be sneaky if she was going to put her plan into action.

The following night, Sunshine was having one of her crying episodes. Stone Woods noticed, and went into the bedroom to 'comfort' her.

"What's wrong, dear?" she asked, trying to conceal the open bottle in her hands just enough so Sunshine wouldn't see.

"I don't know," sobbed Sunshine.

Stone Woods wrapped her in a reassuring hug, holding the bottle underneath Sunshine's chin. Her tears began to trickle into the bottle.

That was all Stone Woods needed for her plan. "Well," she said, "I hope you feel better soon. Bye!" And with that she left Sunshine's house, never to be seen again. Or so she thought.

Back at Stone Woods' castle, she already had an evil brew going. The plan was to make everyone in the kingdom of Netsa even sadder than she was, and Sunshine's tears were the final ingredient she needed. She would fly above the kingdom on her broomstick and sprinkle the potion she'd just concocted over all the people in the kingdom, and they would all immediately feel a wave of depression wash over them. And then Stone Woods would be the happiest person in Netsa.

When Sunshine woke the next morning and stepped outside her house, something did not seem right. The people of the kingdom of Netsa usually seemed bright and cheerful, but today everyone was crying. "What's wrong?" she asked a random passer-by.

"I don't know," the stranger sobbed.

And then Sunshine remembered the conversation she had had with the old lady the previous day. Come to think of it, the old lady looked a little bit familiar...

And then she realised why. The old lady was actually Stone Woods! She'd obviously put a curse on the kingdom of Netsa to make everyone sad. Sunshine raced towards Stone Woods' castle to confront her. She knocked on the door.

"Ah, if it isn't Sunshine Star," Stone Woods said as she opened the door.

"What have you done?" sobbed Sunshine.

"Well, I think you'll find *I'm* the happiest person in the kingdom now!"

"Why have you done this?"

"It was the only way I could be happy."

"Really? Why don't you just talk to someone?" asked Sunshine, desperately.

That made Stone Woods think. Why *didn't* she talk to someone?

She invited Sunshine into the castle. And they talked, for more than two hours, about everything and anything. And by the end Stone Woods was feeling much better, and she agreed to sprinkle the antidote for the sadness potion over the kingdom. Because no one deserved to be sad. And after that day, no one in the kingdom of Netsa ever was again.

THE END

The Autistic Singer

1

"April!"

Even though I had my music up loud, I could still hear my mother loud and clear. Sge banged on my door, so I turned my music down to minimum and opened it.

"April, that music is too loud!"

"I'm sorry," I said.

"I thought you didn't like loud noises?"

I shrugged. "Music is different."

Mum rolled her eyes. "It's late at night, please turn it down!"

"I promise I'll turn it down," I said, and she closed the door. I decided to lower the volume even more, because I had homework to be getting on with. God, I hated school. It wasn't really the subjects - I was always academically advanced - it was the other kids. You see, I was autistic, and I was seen as somewhat 'weird' by the other kids at school. I didn't have that many friends, even though I'd been there ten years.

I opened my backpack and took out my homework. My poor backpack had been through some stuff - namely some of the boys kicking it while it was on my back. I didn't know what was wrong with me, why I was such a target. Obviously it was because I was autistic. I was diagnosed at the age of five. Asperger's syndrome, is what my particular condition is called. Or, at least what it *used* to be called. I don't know why they changed it. Never really looked into it. Never really been bothered by it to be honest.

What *did* bother me was music. OK, that came out wrong. I *loved* music. It was something of a special interest. I was one of those people who could pick out notes a mile off. People were also amazed at how well I could sing. But I'd never had the confidence to do anything about it.

I finished my homework and put it back in my backpack, ready for school the next day. Then I turned my music off and climbed into bed.

###

The major obstacle of any school day was working out where to sit for lunch in the canteen. Everyone had their 'cliques' which left no room for me. I did manage to find a table to myself and I sat there and silently ate my lunch. I was only in the first year, so that meant there was still another five years of the torturous experience to go. I sighed to myself. Life must get easier at some point, I thought to myself.

After lunch I went back to my form room. There was an older girl I didn't recognize in there, standing at the front. I thought that was a little weird, but I sat down anyway.

"This is Jessica," said Mr Carter. "She's here to mentor one of you for the rest of the year.""

Mentor us? Did we need mentoring? I just hoped she wouldn't pick me.

"April," Mr Carter said. "Would you like to be mentored?"

I didn't say anything.

"That's settled then," said Mr Carter. "Jessica, you will be mentoring April."

I rolled my eyes and sighed, Life just kept getting worse.

By Mr Carter's request, I spent lunch break the next day 'getting to know' Jessica.

"Call me Jess," she said. "If you need anything, let me know."

I didn't know what to say.

"So," said Jess, "tell me about yourself."

I hated those words with a passion. What was I meant to say?

"Uh... My name's April and I love music and singing."

Jess nodded. "Very interesting."

I nodded too.

"So have you thought of signing up for a talent show?"

I sighed. "I'm not that confident."

"I'm sure you are," said Jess. "You just need to find that confidence."

I took a deep breath. "There's something else."

"What?"

"I'm autistic."

Jess paused for a moment. "Well, that's OK," she said eventually. "Sounds like you really need a mentor, then."

I shrugged. "I was getting on OK before... Kind of... OK, maybe I do need a mentor."

Jess smiled. "We're going to get on just fine."

###

Jess asked me if I wanted to meet up after school. I'd never been asked to meet up outside of school hours before. She must have really liked me. Either that, or this was some kind of elaborate prank, which I wouldn't be surprised if it was. I wasn't accusing Jess personally, but I was just used to people not liking me for some odd reason.

Jess waited for me to finish at the school gate and then we went to the little ice cream shop in town.

"So," Jess said, "How's school going?"

"Difficult, as usual."

"What's so hard about it?"

I sighed. "The other kids mostly. They think I'm some sort of laughing stock."

"That's not true," said Jess, spooning a scoop of vanilla into her mouth.

"Why do you like me so much?"

"Because you're a nice person, April."

"But don't you think I'm weird?"

"Not really."

"Why can't everyone be like you?"

Jess laughed. "You're sweet."

"Um... thank you, I guess." Compliments made me uncomfortable.

"I'm so glad we're getting to know each other," Jess said.

I paused for a moment. "Me too."

I saw Jess again the next day at school. We had lunch together. It was nice to have someone to sit with at lunch.

"When do I get to hear you sing, then?" asked Jess.

"Oh, I don't really do that in front of anyone," I said, looking down.

"You'll never get anywhere if you never sing in front of anyone."

"Who said I wanted to 'get anywhere'?"

"I just think it would be good for you, April."

I told her I'd think about it. I hoped she wouldn't bring it up again.

###

Jess invited me over to her house the following day. I was nervous about meeting the rest of her family, but still excited to go over to her's.

Her mum was very welcoming when we got in the house.

"Mum, this is April. I've been mentoring her at school."

"Welcome to our home, April," Jess' mum said.

"Hi, thanks for having me," I said, nervously.

"Why don't you girls head upstairs while I prepare dinner?" said Jess' mum.

So we headed upstairs to Jess' room. It was your typical teenage girl's bedroom, with pink walls and stuffed animals on the bed. There was also a computer in the corner of the room.

"So come on then," Jess said, "we're not in public now. Sing to me."

"OK, but it'd be better for me if I didn't look at you."

"OK."

I closed my eyes, took a deep breath and started to sing. I wasn't confident enough to sing much, but Jess seemed to lke it.

"Wow," she said. "I don't think I've ever heard someone sing so good before."

"Really?"

Jess nodded. "I think we should enter you into some kind of talent contest."

"Oh, no, I'm fine."

"Oh, come on, it'll be fun."

"I don't know, Jess."

Suddenly Jess got up off the bed, and headed over to the computer.

"What are you doing?" I asked.

"I'm finding a talent show and entering you."

"Jess, no! Please!"

"Oh, come on. A talent like yours deserves to be discovered. Don't you want a better life, April? This is your ticket!"

I thought for a moment. Jess did have a point. "Go on, then," I said.

Jess quickly found a site for a TV talent show. She brought the form up and I put in all my details.

"Ready?" she asked.

"3...2...1!"

She hit 'submit', and I knew there was nothing more I could do. My application was out there.

Within a few weeks I had all but forgotten about the application to the talent show. That was until I got a phone call from a number I didn't recognize.

"Is that April?" the woman on the other line said.

"That's me," I said.

"I'm calling from the Sing It! auditions team and I'm very pleased to tell you that we'd love you to come and audition for us!"

My stomach did a little flip.

"So, what do you say?"

I hesitated. Yes, it was exciting, for sure, but could I really sing in front of all those people?

"April?"

I decided to go with my gut. "Y-Yes, I'd love to audition for you," I stammered.

"Great. I'll send you an email with all the details. Looking forward to meeting you, April." She hung up.

###

The first thing I did when I got off the phone to the audition people was call Jess.

"I knew they'd accept you!" she squealed. She seemed to be even more excited than I was.

"I'm so nervous," I said.

"You'll do great," she replied.

"Will you come with me?"

"Of course I will," she said.

5

The day of the audition came around and I was no less nervous than before. In fact I think I was even *more* nervous than before. My hands couldn't stop shaking and my heart was racing.

Jess' mum drove us to the TV studio. My mum knew I was going and wished me luck. I hoped having Jess there would calm my nerves a little.

We arrived at the studio, and I was amazed at how big it was. We went inside and I checked myself in, then I was rushed away to have my hair and make-up done. It all seemed so exciting, but I was still nervous.

It was an agonizing wait as I waited for my name to be called to go and audition. But soon enough, my name was called. It was time.

"Good luck," Jess said, giving me a hug.

I stepped inside the audition room, and my nerves went through the roof. I was worried I was going to back out, but I knew I had to do this.

"What's your name?" asked one of the judges.

"April," I stammered.

"Take it away, April."

I took a couple of steps back, took a deep breath, and sang. I sang like I'd never sang before.

When I was done, the judges gave me a round of applause.

"You're good, April. You're really good."

"Thank you," I gushed as the praise continued.

"We'd like to put you through to the next round," said another judge.

"Thank you so much," I squealed. I practically ran out of the audition room towards Jess. I threw my arms around her. "Thank you so much for talking me into this!"

"No problem," she said.

I couldn't stop smiling. I knew it was the start of something big.

The Gold Connection

Amy

"Amy Anderson? The doctor will see you now."

I have never been more nervous in my entire life as I follow the receptionist down the hall to the psychiatrist's office. Mum made this appointment for me because she thinks there's something wrong with me. Cheers, Mum. What she thinks is wrong with me, I have no idea. I'm brought to a small room with a desk and three chairs inside. There's also a plant in the corner and some paintings on the walls.

"Take a seat, Amy," says who I'm assuming is the doc. I do as I'm told.

"Why am I here?" I ask.

"Your mother made this appointment for you," says the doc. She opens a large file and starts to make notes.

"I know that," I say. "But why?"

"To be blunt, Amy, your mother thinks you may be autistic."

"What? Why didn't she tell me?"

"She thought you might be upset."

She's right. I am upset. I'm upset that my own mother thinks there may be something seriously wrong with me.

"Can I ask you some questions, Amy?"

I nod my head, skeptically.

"Amy, do you find communication difficult?"

"Sometimes, I guess. I can't really talk to anyone except my parents."

She scribbles some notes down on the file.

"Do you like set routines?"

These are weird questions.

"I guess so. I get upset if they are interrupted. Well, not upset as such, but a little bit annoyed."

"Do you have any passionate interests?"

"I've always been interested in art. I enjoy being creative."

She continues to write down notes on the file. She continues asking me weird questions for what seems like forever, but is only about half an hour according to the clock on the wall.

Finally, she says, "Thank you, Amy, that's very interesting."

"So? Do you think I have autism?"

"Yes, Amy, I am formally diagnosing you as autistic."

Great. I am officially crazy.

She stands up, holding her hand out to me. "Thank you, Amy, and I hope to see you again soon."

I don't, I think to myself. I shake her hand, reluctantly, and leave the room.

I lay back on my bed and start thinking about my life. So, I have autism. It's not fair. I don't *want* to be autistic. Why me? What did I do to deserve this?

I guess I shouldn't be totally surprised. I've always been a bit quirky.

But being 'quirky' is one thing, having autism is totally another.

Knock knock knock

Suddenly I hear a rapping on my bedroom door. "Come in," I say.

The door opens. It's Mum.

"Just wondering how you got on with the doctor?"

I sit up on the bed. "Well, turns out I have autism. Who'd have thought it?"

Mum's silent for a moment.

Suddenly it hits me. "You've suspected this for a long time, haven't you?"

She sits down on my bed. "I just want you to be able to get the support you need, Amy."

"I don't *need* support. I'm fine."

"I just want you to be OK, Amy."

"Well, like I said, I'm fine."

She pats me on the back, and gets up off the bed. "Just so you know, this doesn't change the way I see you, or anything. I still love you."

I still love you? Where did that come from? I don't think I've ever heard my mother tell me she loves me.

I lay back on the bed again, sigh, and bring my pillow up to my face.

I'm sat on the couch, watching *Frozen* for the millionth time. It's my five-year-old daughter Connie's favorite movie. I know all the words by heart, because Connie likes to watch this movie over and over again, multiple times a day.

You might think this is strange, or you might think it's just Connie being a typical child. It's neither. Every time Connie watches *Frozen* it's like she's watching it for the first time. Because Connie is autistic. And so am I. I got diagnosed when I was twelve. Back then my condition was known as Asperger's syndrome. Shortly after I had Connie, she started portraying some of the traits I had when I was younger, so I got her tested. Connie was diagnosed a year ago.

"Is she watching that *again?*" My husband Phil comes in from work. Phil isn't autistic - he's neurotypical - but he deals with mine and Connie's ways really well.

"It's an autistic thing," I explain.

Phil shrugs, and goes to the kitchen to pour a cup of coffee.

I lean over the side of the sofa and reach for my iPad. I love the Internet. It gives me a chance to interact with people that I may not have in the outside world. Being autistic means that I struggle to communicate in real life, and so the Internet is great because it's much easier to communicate. I like Facebook and Twitter the best. I'm in several autistic groups on Facebook. They're a great support for me. Without the Internet, I wouldn't have been as accepting of my condition as I am. I found a whole community of autistics, and they gave me the confidence to be myself.

There's not much happening on the autistic groups today, so I close my iPad and go back to watching the movie. When I said I knew all the words, I didn't just mean the songs; I mean I literally know every single word of the film. But Connie likes it, and in some ways it helps her cope, so I put up with it for her.

Then suddenly, I clock the time. Five thirty. Already? I swear it was only three the last time I looked. Time for me to prepare dinner.

I get up off the couch and head into the kitchen.

Amy

I've been sulking in my room for the past five days. I haven't left my room apart from for school. I don't think I'll ever accept the fact that I have autism. It doesn't feel right to me.

Suddenly Mum comes into my room, with tea and biscuits. "I thought I might cheer you up," she says, sitting down on my bed.

"Well, you failed," I say.

She puts her hand on my back. "Look, I know things are a little overwhelming right now, but things will get better, I promise."

"I just don't like being different," I say, sadly.

"Well, there are lots of people like you. I'll bet if you go online you could find some."

I just sigh deeply.

Mum pats me on the back and gets up off the bed. "I'm always here if you need me, Amy." She walks out the door and closes it behind her.

As she leaves I sigh once more. Things have *got* to get better for me.

One thing she said sticks out to me though. What if I *could* find other people like me online?

I pick my laptop off the side of my bed and fire it up. Then I navigate to Facebook. In the search bar I type *'group for autistic people'*. Loads of results come up. I click on the first one, join up, and once I've been accepted, I make a new post.

Amy Anderson:

Hi. I've recently been diagnosed with autism and I feel a bit overwhelmed. I'm hoping to find some friends and support in this group. It would be great if someone could reach out to me.

Did that last part sound too needy? Well, I've hit 'send' now, so it's too late.

Beth

Dinner has been eaten and now we're all sat down on the couch together. Connie has already restarted *Frozen* again after finishing it earlier this afternoon. To say I'm a little bored is an understatement. I pick up my iPad and start scrolling through the autism groups again.

I see there's a new post been added by a girl called Amy Anderson:

Amy Anderson:

Hi. I've recently been diagnosed with autism and I feel a bit overwhelmed. I'm hoping to find some friends and support in this group. It would be great if someone could reach out to me.

I don't normally reply to newbies asking for support, but since she asked for someone to reach out to her, I decide to reply.

Beth Williams:

Hi Amy. You can send me a message if you like.

I close my iPad, thinking nothing more about it, and fall asleep on the couch.

When I wake, sure enough, there's a message from Amy Anderson.

Amy Anderson:

Hi. Thanks for reaching out to me.

Beth Williams:

You're welcome. How are you?

Amy Anderson:

Not good. I'm so confused.

Beth Williams:

What are you confused about?

Amy Anderson:

So many things. I don't want to be autistic.

Poor girl. I was like that when I first got diagnosed. I didn't want to be 'different'. Now, thanks to people online, I've embraced the identity.

Amy Anderson:

How do I accept myself?

Beth Williams:

I can help you with that, if you want. But it will take some time.

I press 'enter' before I even have a
chance to think about what I'm saying.
What have I gotten myself in for?

Amy Anderson:

You would? That would be great!

Great.

Amy

The next day I struggle through
school again. I guess my diagnosis
explains why I find learning so difficult.

When I get home and log on,
Beth is already online. I decide to get to
know her a little better.

Amy Anderson:

Tell me about yourself.

Beth Williams:

Uh... I'm thirty years old, I have a daughter called Connie, and I'm happily married.

Wow. If Beth can have a successful life while having autism, why shouldn't I?

Amy Anderson:

I'm fifteen. I'm in school at the moment. Never dated anyone.

Beth Williams:

That's cool. You have plenty of time to date.

Amy Anderson:

Do you think I will?

Beth Williams:

I don't know you that well, so I can't say. I don't see why autism would stop you though.

That gives me a bit more confidence.

Amy Anderson:

How did you come to terms with having autism?

Beth Williams:

Firstly, in the autistic community, we prefer to say we 'are autistic', rather than we 'have autism'. It's because autism is not an accessory that we can take off; it's intertwined in our very being. Everything about me is autistic, the same way everything about you is autistic.

OK. I'm learning things here. It's good to learn, especially if I want to fit in with the autistic community.

Beth Williams:

But to answer your question, it was the online community that helped me accept myself for who I was. Without them, I would be very unsure of myself, like you are now.

I guess it's good to know I'm not alone.

Amy Anderson:

I hope with your help I will be able to accept myself too.

Beth Williams:

You don't need me to help you accept yourself.

Amy Anderson:

But I do. I need someone to help me.

Do I sound a bit needy? I have got to stop sounding needy when I chat to people.

Beth Williams:

Well, I've got to go and see to my daughter.

Amy Anderson:

OK, chat to you later!

Beth Williams:

Bye!

And with that she's gone.

Beth is such a nice person for reaching out and talking to me.

Man, I hope I don't get *too* attached.

Beth

Connie gets dropped home from school the next day at three fifteen. She's not herself tonight. She doesn't want to talk to me, and tell me how her day's gone.

"Connie?" I ask, "is everything OK?"

"I hate school," she grumbles.

It's at that moment that it hits me. Connie obviously had a meltdown at school for some reason. Literally anything can set her off, but it's mostly when she's finding her learning difficult. I used to have a lot of meltdowns at school. And I was always wondering why my way of dealing with things - or lack thereof - was so different from the other kids. That's until I got my diagnosis when I was twelve. It answered a lot of questions, but it also made me feel ashamed because I was different.

I try to put my arms around her, but she backs away. Connie dislikes being touched, but only when she's stressed out.

I watch her as she marches up the stairs to her room, slamming the door behind her.

I don't bother going after her; I know she needs time alone.

I decide to turn my attention to my little 'pet project' I have going on. Amy. I roll my eyes. I don't really have time to mentor some kid, but that's what I've signed myself up for. I tell myself I can back out at any time. I pick up my iPad, in the hope she won't be online. I have dinner to be getting on with. But sure enough, there's a green light by Amy's name. Fantastic.

Amy Anderson:

Hi Beth. Can I chat to you for a minute?

Beth Williams:

Sure thing.

Sometimes I think I'm too nice for my own good.

Amy Anderson:

How did you feel when you got diagnosed?

Beth Williams:

At the time I was devastated, but the online community has since helped me reclaim my identity.

Amy Anderson:

How long did it take you to accept yourself?

Beth Williams:

Well, let's see... I first joined the online community when I was your age, so about three years.

Amy Anderson:

And how did that help you?

She's very inquisitive, isn't she?

Beth Williams:

I guess I felt OK because there were other people out there like myself.

Amy Anderson:

Sadly, I don't think I know enough about autism to be able to accept myself.

Does she think I'm Google or something?

I'm not getting in too deep in this. I'll talk to her, but that's that.

Beth Williams:

There should be some information at your school if you ask.

Amy Anderson:

Thanks for the advice!

"Mommy!"

That would be Connie calling for me. I have to go see what she wants.

Beth Williams:

Got to go now. My daughter needs me.

Amy Anderson:

OK, chat tomorrow!

Oh, God, really?

She really has turned into my pet project. I don't have time for this; I'm a busy mom.

Amy

Following Beth's advice I am now sat outside the headmaster's office twiddling my thumbs and feeling nervous as hell. I've never been to the headmaster's office before. I don't think I've even met the headmaster. I hate having to meet new people. It gives me major anxiety.

Finally the headmaster opens the door to his office and leads me inside. "What can I do for you, Amy?" he asks as we sit down.

"Well, I've recently been diagnosed with - I mean, as autistic, and I'm a bit confused about things. I was wondering if the school had any info on the subject?"

He goes over to the filing cabinet in the corner of the room, opens one of the drawers, and pulls out a bunch of leaflets.

"Read these," he says, handing them to me. "They should give you all the information you need."

I consider the leaflets carefully. A few of them have a puzzle piece symbol on them. I'm guessing that's the symbol for autism.

"Thank you," I say, grabbing the leaflets and heading out the door.

When I get home from school I quickly log on to my laptop in the hopes that Beth is online. Luckily she is.

Amy Anderson:

Hi Beth.

Beth Williams:

Hi. How did it go at school?

Amy Anderson:

OK, I guess. I got a bunch of leaflets on autism. Most of them have this puzzle piece symbol on them. I'm guessing that's the symbol for autism?

She takes a little while to reply this time.

Beth Williams:

It's hard to explain.

Amy Anderson:

I've got the time.

Beth Williams:

The puzzle piece is a symbol for autism, but most autistics view the puzzle piece as problematic.

Amy Anderson:

Why's that?

Beth Williams:

Because it implies that autistic people have a piece missing. We don't. We are whole human beings that think differently to others.

Wow. I guess some autistic people have a lot of time on their hands.

She links me to an article about why the puzzle piece is problematic. I have a good read of the article.

Amy Anderson:

Anything else I should know?

Beth Williams:

About autism? Where do I start?

I guess this 'community' is a lot more complicated than I first thought.

Beth Williams:

I need to see to my daughter, I'll talk to you another time.

Disappointment rushes through me, but I accept that Beth's a busy mum.

Amy Anderson:

OK, chat tomorrow?

Beth Williams:

Maybe. Bye!

She logs off.

I decide to do a little research for myself about the autistic community. Then next time she's online I can impress her with

Beth

I wake the next morning to the sound of Connie making random noises. She does this because it's part of her stimming rituals. Stimming is exactly what it sounds like - behavior that stimulates you.

"Connie?" I call out. "Are you OK?"

Connie doesn't respond and continues making her noises.

I roll over and grab my iPad. Amy is online. Does she ever log off?

Beth Williams:

Hi Amy.

Amy Anderson:

Hi Beth. I've done a little research on the autistic community.

Well, at least she's showing her own initiative.

Beth Williams:

That's great. What have you found?

Amy Anderson:

I found out that the infinity symbol is preferred by autistics.

Beth Williams:

That's true.

Amy Anderson:

And I found out about Autism Speaks.

Beth Williams:

Ah yes. Autism $peaks.

Amy Anderson:

Huh?

She obviously didn't look hard enough.

Beth Williams:

That's how we refer to AS in the autistic community.

Amy Anderson:

OK. Well, I think Autism $peaks is pretty terrible.

Beth Williams:

You are correct.

Amy Anderson:

I also found out about #LightItUpGold.

Beth Williams:

See? You don't need me anymore.

Amy Anderson:

But I do. You're my friend.

Aw. She thinks I'm her friend.

Well, she's wrong. I don't have time to be her friend.

I also can't bring myself to tell her I don't have time to be her friend.

We'll just have to wait and see what happens.

Amy

I can't sleep. I lay awake in my bed, tossing and turning. I can't stop thinking about Beth. I think I'm growing too attached to her.

I get out of bed, grab my computer and navigate to my chat with

Beth. The time zone is different where she is, so luckily she's online.

Amy Anderson:

Hi Beth. Can you chat?

She takes a little while to reply.

Beth Williams:

Sure I can. What's up?

Amy Anderson:

I just wanted to thank you for helping me through my diagnosis.

Beth Williams:

No problem. Glad to be of help.

Amy Anderson:

I'd like to meet you one day.

Beth Williams:

I don't think that's such a good idea.

Amy Anderson:

Why not?

Beth Williams:

The only thing we really have in common is autism.

Amy Anderson:

But I don't know anyone else who's autistic. I need you in my life.

Beth Williams:

You don't need me. You'll do great on your own.

And that's when it hits me. I'm my own person. Yes, I'm autistic, but that's only part of who I am.

Amy Anderson:

Thanks again, Beth. I don't think I need you any more after all.

Beth Williams:

I told you so. You'll do great.

The Singcreek Mermaid

Singcreek was a small town on the outskirts of San Ceanseph. It was a normal town, full of normal people. But not everyone in Singcreek was normal. Savannah Stein and her family had recently moved to Singcreek, and Savannah was making a *splash* at Singcreek High.

Savannah had never been to a regular school before. In fact, she'd never been in a regular town before either. Because Savannah was a mermaid.

Now, Savannah didn't go around flapping her tail about in school. She didn't have a tail while she was in school; she had legs like a regular person. It was difficult for her to get used to walking on legs because she'd spent most of her time in the sea. Why did she move to a regular town, instead of staying in the sea, you ask? Her parents wanted her to get an education. Her parents had high hopes for their daughter.

Savannah had had the weekend to practice her walking before school started. But by the time Monday came she *still* didn't quite have the hang of it. Never mind, she thought. The other kids probably wouldn't take much notice of her walking.

Except they did.

"Are you OK?" asked Lisa one morning as they were going to school.

"What do you mean?" asked Savannah.

"If you don't mind me saying, you walk a little... awkwardly."

"Oh, right. I have a condition... thing... that makes me walk weird."

But Lisa didn't look too convinced.

Suddenly they stopped outside Savannah's classroom door.

"This is me," said Savannah. "Bye!" And she disappeared.

Lisa was left feeling more confused than ever.

After a couple of days, Savannah felt like she had almost mastered walking on legs. She hoped no one else would notice her stumbling around. She wanted to keep her true identity a secret, because she didn't want the attention.

Everything would be fine, so long as she didn't get her legs wet.

Unfortunately for Savannah, the next day was Swim Class Day.

Savannah gave her teacher a note that excused her from swim class. The note also excused her from being poolside. But the rest of the class couldn't stop talking about her.

"Where did she transfer from?" asked Eric.

"I hear she's from the city," said Molly.

But the gossiping didn't get Savannah down. It made her laugh slightly, but it didn't get her down.

Savannah was walking with her books to her next class, when she bumped into Travis - literally. Her books went everywhere.

"I'm so sorry," said Travis.

"No, it's fine," said Savannah. She looked into his eyes. They were a beautiful sparkling blue. Savannah felt her stomach do a little flip. She'd never felt like this before - none of the mermen under the sea had never taken her fancy. But this? This was different.

"Uh...." Travis was lost for words.

"Are you OK?"

"Yeah, yeah I'm fine." Travis ruffled his hair.

Savannah was just about to continue walking to her class when Travis stopped her. "What are you doing this Friday?"

"Nothing, I don't think. Why?"

"Would you like to come to the school dance with me?"

Savannah had forgotten about the school dance. She wasn't going to go, but now that Travis has asked her, she'd changed her mind.

"Sure," Savannah smiled.

"Cool. I'll pick you up at seven."

The bell rang, and Savannah hurried to her next class. And she couldn't stop smiling.

Savannah spent hours contemplating what to wear. In the end she chose a blue strapless dress, as a nod to her life n the sea. She hoped the color wouldn't give any clues to her identity.

But at the same time, she really liked Travis, and felt like she should tell him about her identity. But also, she felt she wasn't quite ready yet.

It was a lot to think about.

Travis picked up Savannah at seven on the dot. Savannah felt she was excited about the night ahead. She'd never been to a dance before - of course. She'd never been to a real school before this week.

"You look amazing," said Travis when he clapped eyes on Savannah.

"Thank you," Savannah said, trying not to blush too hard.

They got in the limo, which took them to the school. Hundreds of people were there. Savannah had never seen a place so busy before.

After dancing and mingling for a few hours, Travis said, "Let's go outside."

The went outside to the courtyard. "Having fun?" asked Travis.

Savannah nodded. This was it, she thought. This was the moment she was going to tell Travis her big secret.

"I wanted to show you something," said Savannah. Nervously, she splashed some water from the fountain onto her legs. They transformed into a mermaid tail.

Travis could hardly speak. He was in shock.

"Travis," Savannah said, "say something!"

"You're a mermaid?"

"Uh-huh." *This is the part where he runs away,* Savannah thought to herself, sadly.

But he didn't run away. "That's.... so cool," he said.

"You like it?"

"I love it." He kissed Savannah, and it felt magical.

They spent the rest of the evening sitting outside in the courtyard.

It was the best night of Savannah's life.

www.ingramcontent.com/pod-product-compliance
Lightning Source LLC
Chambersburg PA
CBHW030318160726
47992CB00005B/2057